THIS BOOK BELONGS TO:

----

igloobooks

Published in 2017
by Igloo Books Ltd
Cottage Farm
Sywell
NN6 0BJ
www.igloobooks.com

Written by Melanie Joyce
Interiors illustrated by Adam Horsepool

Designed by Alex Alexandrou
Edited by Mike Heron

With special thanks to Psyop

GRA005 1117
2 4 6 8 10 9 7 5 3 1
ISBN 978-1-78810-999-4

Printed and manufactured in EU

Kevin the carrot was so excited. He couldn't believe his eyes.

In this year's Christmas competition, he'd won a special prize.

It was a golden ticket, for a ride on Santa's train,

to the North Pole for Christmas, and then back home again.

Kevin packed his suitcase
and soon it was time to leave.
The Santa train was waiting
at the station on Christmas Eve.

"**Wow,**" said Kevin, smiling. His dreams were coming true.
Then a voice behind him said, "**I won a ticket, too!**"

"Hello, my name is Katie. Aren't we the luckiest carrots ever.
We're actually going to meet Santa. We'll remember this forever."

Kevin felt so happy. Now there was someone to share the fun.

"All aboard!" cried the conductor. **"Quick,"** said Kevin, **"run!"**

They giggled as they
jumped on board.
The great train
slowly chuffed.
It clicked and clacked
along the track, as
it pulled and puffed.

Little stars were twinkling in the soft moonlight,
as the Santa train went North on that magical night.

Santa's train was everything the carrots thought it would be.

There was tinsel and fairy lights, and a glittering Christmas tree.

"Look," said Katie, **"warm mince pies and little snacks and sweets."**

The carrots couldn't resist and ate lots of delicious treats.

Then something funny happened. Next door they heard a sound.

Peeping round the carriage door, what do you think they found?

There was Mrs Claus trying to calm down Santa's elves, who were completely over-excited, and swinging from the shelves!

Santa sat with his feet up and so did his reindeer, too.

Mrs Claus was not impressed and said, **"It's alright for you!"**

Santa twiddled his beard and said, **"I'm rather tired you know.**

Being Santa Claus is exhausting. I'm always on the go!"

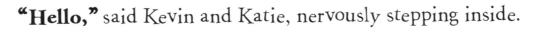

"Hello," said Kevin and Katie, nervously stepping inside.

"Welcome on board," said Santa, **"I hope we haven't spoiled the ride."**

"**Christmas can be stressful,**" he said. "**Do forgive us please,**"

just as a little elf swung by on a tinsel trapeze.

"**Let's get some snacks,**" said Kevin. "**They might improve the mood,**"

but the reindeer charged at the carrots and gobbled up all the food.

"Let's play games," said Kevin. "There are loads of them in this sack."

"Good idea!" said the elves, as the train clattered down the track.

Mrs Claus sang karaoke, and everyone else joined in.

The reindeer put on their earmuffs, it was such an awful din.

Soon, everyone was laughing. They'd forgotten how grumpy they'd been.

Because Santa doing a jig was the funniest thing they'd ever seen.

Then, something amazing happened. Katie cried, **"Look out there!"**

Santa's train had taken off and was flying through the air.

"**Hurray!**" shouted a little elf. "**Because of the Christmas cheer,**
we'll definitely get to the North Pole an awful lot faster this year."

The reindeer jingled their bells. They wanted to go flying, too.

"**Oh, alright,**" said Santa. "**It will be good practice for you.**"

The elves had so much fun making snowballs out of snow,
and chucking them at the reindeer as they flew down below.

The train whizzed past the stars and swooped down to the land.

"I feel a bit dizzy," said Kevin, holding Katie's hand.

The lights of the frosty North Pole soon came into sight.

"Time to land," said the conductor. **"Everyone hold on tight!"**

All the work was done and the elves filled Santa's sack.

Then Mrs Claus and Santa climbed into the back.

Santa said to Kevin and Katie,

"I've got a surprise for you.

You are flying the sleigh tonight,

and delivering the presents, too."

"Hurray!" cried the carrots, as

they whizzed off in the sleigh.

It was definitely going to be the

most amazing Christmas day.

Mrs Claus and Santa smiled. **"Merry Christmas, ho-ho-ho."**

As Kevin and Katie giggled, and hugged under the mistletoe.